bertha
and the Great Painting Job

Story by **Eric Charles**
Pictures by **Steve Augarde**

from the original television designs by **Ivor Wood**

From the BBC TV Series

ANDRE DEUTSCH

First published in 1985 by
André Deutsch Limited
105 Great Russell Street London WC1B 3LJ

British Library Cataloguing in Publication Data

Charles, Eric
  Bertha and the great painting job.
  I. Title II. Augarde, Steve III. Wood, Ivor
  823'.914[J]   PZ7

ISBN 0–233–97813–5

It was a busy morning at Spottiswood and Company. Upstairs, Mr Willmake, the manager, was getting ready for the decorators. Miss McClackerty, his secretary, was helping him cover the furniture with sheets.

Downstairs in the factory Bertha, the big machine, was making jigsaw puzzles.

Ted put the picture in at one end and Bertha cut out the shapes.
Nell was packing the puzzles into boxes and Flo was stacking them.

Roy went over to the conveyor belt to check that all was well.

Suddenly a puzzle came through with a piece missing. He held it up. "You'd better stop Bertha, Ted," he called, "there's something wrong here."

Ted stopped the machine and came to look. "Mmmm," he said, "it must still be inside." He climbed on to Bertha and poked his head inside to see if he could see it. "Nothing there," he called back and got down.

"Try putting another picture through," said Nell, "It might push the missing piece out."

Everyone waited. When the puzzle arrived, it too had a piece missing.

"It's part of the sky," said Roy, pointing to a hole in the picture.

"What's she up to?" said Ted.

"Very mysterious," said Nell.

"Very puzzling," said Flo.

"I think Bertha's keeping pieces to make a puzzle of her own," said Roy.

Ted patted Bertha affectionately. "Now, come on, Bertha," he coaxed, "let's have those missing pieces."

A clinking sound came from deep inside the machine. Her lights flashed and her cogs turned. With a "Clonk" and a "Clatter" she sent out the missing pieces – lots of them – neatly fitted together.

Ted looked at the pattern Bertha had made. "A very clever piece of work," he said. "I reckon, that to make this, Bertha must have kept back a piece from almost every puzzle we've made this morning."

He pointed to the stack of boxes at the end of the conveyor belt. "We'll have to make up all these puzzles to find out which pieces are missing."

Roy let out a short sharp whistle. "It'll take ages."

"We'd better get started then," said Ted, "We can't have the shops selling puzzles with pieces missing, can we?"

Flo handed Nell a box from the top of the stack. "It's better than stacking," she said.

Nell emptied the box on to the packing table and began to sort out the pieces. "It's better than packing," she said.

Ted looked at Bertha and shook his head. "Bertha, how could you?" he scolded. Bertha made a noise that almost sounded like – "Sorry".

Upstairs, in the office, Mr Willmake looked at his watch. "Those decorators are late," he said, "I wonder where they've got to?"

He stood, with Miss McClackerty, in the middle of the room; everything around them was covered in white sheets. The telephone rang.

"That sounds like the telephone, sir," said Miss McClackerty.

"It does, Miss McClackerty, but where is it?"

Miss McClackerty thought for a moment. The telephone went on ringing. "When I cleared the desk, I think I put it on the floor – somewhere," she said.

"Well, we've got to find it," said Mr Willmake, "the call may be important."

They went in different directions around the room, treading carefully on the white sheets. The telephone rang and rang.

Miss McClackerty got more and more worried. "Where can it be?" she said.

"Don't panic," said Mr Willmake. "I've got a plan." He picked up the end of a sheet. "I will go under the sheet at this end you go under it from your end. Whoever finds the telephone first, answers it – agreed?"

Miss McClackerty nodded; she got down on her hands and knees and crawled under the sheet. Mr Willmake did the same from his end.

When Mrs Tupp, the tea-lady, came into the office, she saw two bumps moving around the room under white sheets. One of the bumps stopped and sat up. Mr Willmake's voice came from under the sheet, "I've found it."

The telephone stopped ringing. "Hello?" said Mr Willmake. The other bump moved towards him. "Thank you," said Mr Willmake, and put down the telephone. The other bump asked, "Who was it, sir?"

"The decorators. They're not coming."

"Whatever shall we do?" asked Miss McClackerty.

"I'm afraid we'll have to do it ourselves," said Mr Willmake. "Don't worry, I'll think of something."

"If there is anybody in this room, would they like a nice cup of tea?" asked Mrs Tupp from the doorway.

Startled, the two bumps jumped up quickly. Still draped in sheets they looked even funnier.

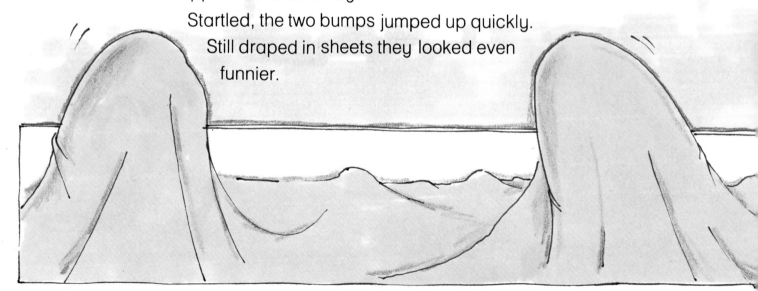

"Yes, please, Mrs Tupp,"
they said together.

Downstairs, Mr Duncan, the factory foreman, came by.

"What's all this," he said, peering over Ted's shoulder, "Playtime?"

"We're not playing, we are looking for missing pieces," explained Ted.

"And why are the pieces missing?" asked the foreman.

"We think Bertha must be making her own puzzles," Roy told him.

"Ah! Been misbehaving, has she?" Mr Duncan turned to Bertha.

"Been misbehaving, have you?"

Bertha began to make loud clanking sounds. She didn't like the foreman.

"Well, if Bertha likes making jigsaws, why don't you put them all back inside her and let her sort them out?" said Mr Duncan.

"Now why didn't I think of that?" said Ted.

"Because that's what a foreman is for," said Mr Duncan.

"I hope he won't make trouble for Bertha," said Nell.

"He can't if we get her to find the missing pieces," said Ted. "Come on, put all the puzzles back inside her and I'll work out a new programme."

In another office Mr Sprott, the designer, was working on a new plan for a painting machine specially ordered by Mr Willmake. Tracy, his assistant and computer programmer, watched him. Mr Sprott put down his set square. "That should do it," he said, looking at the finished drawing.

"Will it work, Mr Sprott?" asked Tracy.

"Undoubtedly." Mr Sprott never had any doubts about his designs. "I'll take this drawing down to the Bumper and Grinder machine and have it made."

"Do you mind if I have a go at designing a machine?" Tracy asked.

Mr Sprott turned and smiled at her. "Of course not," he said, "Have a go if you want to, but mine is the one that will work."

Tracy sat down at the drawing board and sharpened her pencil. "What this factory really needs," she said to herself, "is an all-purpose robot. A friendly intelligent machine." She began to draw. "A machine that can paint, fetch and carry and do all the odd jobs around the factory." The robot began to take shape on the paper in front of her. "I'll get Bertha to make it," she said using her computer to work out the difficult bits. This was going to be a special robot, so she couldn't afford to make any mistakes.

By the time Tracy arrived downstairs with her designs Bertha had just finished sorting out the missing pieces of puzzle.

"Hello, Tracy," said Ted, "What can I do for you?"

Tracy gave him the drawings. "Do you think Bertha can make this?"

"Bertha can make anything," said Ted. He unrolled the drawings and looked at them. "Phew! A robot!" he exclaimed.

Roy came to look. "Bertha will enjoy making that," he said.

Ted took the drawings to the computer panel and pulled the start lever; Bertha's lights flashed and her cogs turned; "Clonk – Clink – Clatter" she went. Ted smiled. "Yes," he said, "Bertha's going to enjoy making a robot."

Upstairs Mr Sprott's newly made painting machine was doing very well. It had two arms with a paint roller on the end of each; as one painted, the other picked up fresh paint from a tray. Panjid, who was very good with mechanical things, was operating it. "This is a fine invention of yours, Mr Sprott," he said, as he moved it along the wall.

Mr Willmake was delighted. "I'm glad those decorators didn't turn up," he said, "or we wouldn't have this fine machine."

Miss McClackerty agreed. "Yes," she said, "and it's so fast. You will stop it at the door, won't you, Panjid. I don't want a yellow door."

Panjid pushed the lever to stop the machine, but nothing happened. He pushed down as hard as he could. The machine went on painting. "I fear something has gone wrong," he said. "This fine machine is behaving badly and will result in Miss McClackerty having a yellow door."

"Do something, Panjid!" cried Miss McClackerty." "I do not want a yellow door!"

"Certainly, Miss McClackerty. When the machine gets to the door, I will open it, and then there will be nothing to paint."

As the machine's arm swung down to paint the door, Panjid opened it.
Unfortunately – at the very moment Mr Duncan arrived. The paint roller ran
smoothly over him, covering him from hat to toe in yellow paint.

"Turn the machine off, Panjid!" cried Mr Sprott. "Push the lever down hard!"
Panjid ran to the machine. "This is what I have been trying to do," he
said, "I shall move the lever in the other direction." He pushed the lever up.
"NO. DON'T DO THAT!" cried Mr Sprott, frantically. But it was too late.

The speed of the machine increased ten fold; the paint rollers whizzed,
painting everything in sight.
"Under the sheets!" shouted Mr Willmake, and everyone dived for cover.

The machine went faster and faster, yellow paint flying in all directions. It painted everything; the walls, the floors, the ceiling – even the window. Everyone huddled together under the sheet. "What shall we do?" said Miss McClackerty. "We can't hide here all day."

"I'm afraid we will have to until the machine runs out of paint," Mr Sprott told her. "Oh, dear!" he sighed, "I must have got something wrong. I hope Tracy's doing better."

Downstairs everyone was crowded around Bertha. Suddenly, with a "Peep–Peep" a little robot came out on to the conveyor belt, eyes flashing and arms swinging, looking very important. "Peep–Peep" it went again.

"Is this what you wanted, Tracy?" asked Ted, as the robot was lifted on to the floor.

Tracy looked at it. "It's just as I designed it," she said. "I will call it TOM. T–O–M. Talk Operated Machine, because you will be able to tell it what to do."

"Will it be able to help me pack?" said Nell.
"And will it be able to help me stack?" asked Flo.

"Yes," said Tracy, "It will even help Roy to sweep up. Won't you, TOM?"
The little robot turned in a tight circle. "Peep—Peep," it answered.

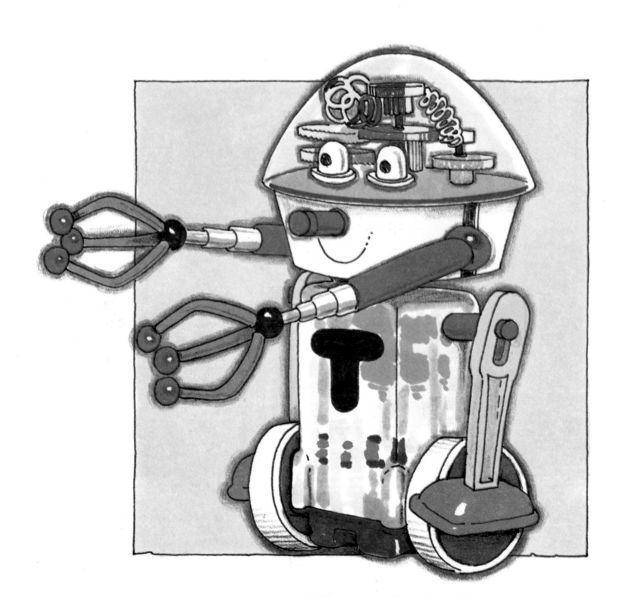

Mr Willmake and Mr Sprott arrived, red faced and splattered with paint.
"Will it be able to paint the factory?" asked Mr Willmake.

"TOM will be able to do anything you ask him," said Tracy proudly. "He's talk operated. Just give him a pot of paint and a brush and you'll see."

"Well done, Tracy." Mr Sprott congratulated her.
"Well done, *Bertha*," said Ted, "you made him."